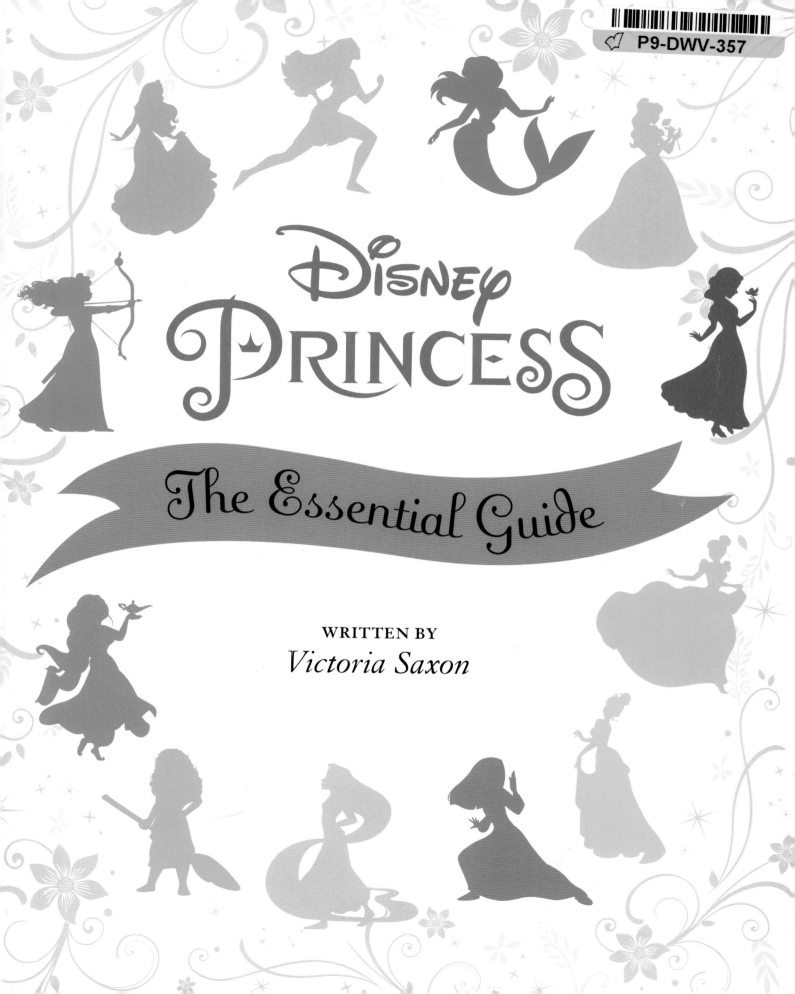

Disney
Princess

The Essential Guide

WRITTEN BY
Victoria Saxon

Contents

Introduction

By royal decree, you are cordially invited to visit some far-off lands and meet twelve incredible princesses. Be prepared for tales of magic spells, amazing courage, and loyal friendships. The princesses are daring and tenacious, strong and brave, kind and curious. And while they have all faced challenges that seem impossible to overcome, they are always willing to step up to find a way through. They face down foes, conquer villains, and try their best to help others in need. In the end, you will find that these princesses are always the heroines of their own stories.

The princesses

Snow White
This kind and gentle soul shows that it's the beauty on the inside that is important.

Cinderella
Even when her life is difficult, Cinderella is forever hopeful that happiness is not far away. She is right!

Aurora
Aurora may have been born into royalty, but she doesn't know it. Her grace and strength are what make her a true princess.

Ariel
She trades in her fins to learn about human life on land. But Ariel risks all to save the ones she loves.

Jasmine

The daughter of the Sultan is open-minded and generous to everyone she meets. And she isn't afraid to stand up for what she believes in.

Belle

She loves to read, but Belle's own adventure has more exciting twists and turns than any of her favorite books.

Pocahontas

Pocahontas wants to understand people who are different from her. Her love of peace helps save her own people from a war.

Mulan

Though she has a hard time fitting in, Mulan's cleverness and determination help her save China.

Moana

Moana's heart is with her family, but the idea of an ocean adventure is too strong for her to resist.

Rapunzel

Rapunzel makes the most of her time trapped inside her tower. But when she finally sets foot outside, it is time to have some fun.

Merida

She fights for her freedom, but Merida soon learns the meaning of true bravery and mends her broken family bonds.

Tiana

Tiana has big dreams for her future, and she's willing to work hard to make them come true.

Snow White

Snow White lives with her wicked stepmother, the cruel Queen. When the Magic Mirror tells the Queen that Snow White is surpassing her in beauty, Snow White must flee to the forest. Her life is in danger—until she finds seven little friends to help her!

About Snow White

★ She's sweet and gentle and she makes lots of friends wherever she goes.

★ She is nurturing and caring to all around her.

★ She is optimistic, and she sees the good in every situation.

Working hard

It seems like Snow White's wish for love will never come true. She's too busy spending all of her time working hard for the Queen.

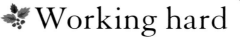

Snow White's clothes are simple but practical.

Animal friends

The animals and birds of the forest love Snow White's kind and gentle nature. She is a friend to all creatures, and she has a habit of finding new friends!

Her hair is as black as ebony.

Her lips are as red as roses.

🌿 Her favorite things

Singing and dancing always cheers Snow White up and gives her courage when she's afraid. The Dwarfs are delighted to dance with her, even if they have to stand on each other's shoulders to be tall enough dance partners!

Snow White loves to go out into the forest with her animal friends. She even finds some berries to make the Seven Dwarfs' favorite pie!

Everything's going to be alright.

Long skirt is perfect for dancing.

🌿 Captivating

A young prince passes by the castle and hears Snow White's singing. He is mesmerized by the sound of her lovely voice.

Enchanted world

For her entire life, Snow White has lived in a vast and beautiful kingdom. Beyond the farthest hill stands the castle where she grew up with her vain and wicked stepmother, the Queen. In the midst of the forest, she finds a new home in the Seven Dwarfs' cottage.

The wishing well where Snow White dreams about her future

Running away

After she runs away from the Queen and the Huntsman, Snow White soon faces the frightening trees in the forest.

The Queen's laboratory and dungeons lie below the castle.

Snow White has nowhere to go and gets lost in the dense forest. Eventually, she can run no further, and she falls to the ground in tears.

The clearing where Snow White meets the friendly forest animals

Every day, the Seven Dwarfs march off into the hills near their cottage. They work hard all day long in the sparkling diamond mines.

A different life

Snow White finds her happy ending with her true love, far away from the wicked Queen.

The Prince's castle

Entrance to the mines

The forest where Snow White sleeps after she is poisoned

The Dwarfs' cottage

The cottage

The Seven Dwarfs are not very good at keeping their home clean and tidy! Snow White hopes to surprise them and cleans the cottage with some help from her loyal animal friends.

Friends and enemies

One of Snow White's great gifts is her ability to make friends. The animals and Dwarfs would do anything for her—even Grumpy! But the Queen is madly jealous of her naturally beautiful stepdaughter. And the cruel Queen is a very dangerous enemy to have.

Secret enemy

As well as being Snow White's stepmother, the Queen is also a wicked witch. She hates Snow White so much that she uses a poisoned apple to try to get rid of her.

Though she is beautiful on the outside, the Queen has an evil heart.

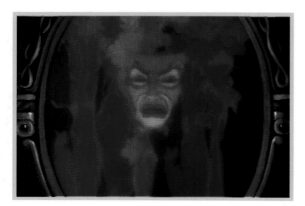

The Magic Mirror must truthfully answer the jealous Queen's questions about Snow White.

Magic Mirror on the wall, who is the fairest one of all?

Before turning red, for a moment, the apple reveals the poison that covers it.

Although the Huntsman is a loyal servant of the Queen, he is not wicked. Seeing Snow White's sweet nature, he cannot bear to carry out the Queen's order to kill the innocent princess.

🍃 Her friends

The Seven Dwarfs and the animals that meet Snow White love her dearly. They try to protect her from the wicked Queen and her evil spells.

Happy   Grumpy   Sneezy   Dopey   Sleepy   Bashful

Doc

Each Dwarf has a strong and special personality, and Snow White sees the best in each one.

A wish comes true

From the moment that Snow White becomes more beautiful than the Queen, she is in danger. Although the Seven Dwarfs try their best, they cannot protect her from the Queen's magic. But good is stronger than evil, and so Snow White always believes that things will work out in the end.

One spring morning

What starts out as just another day ends up changing the course of Snow White's life forever. It all begins when the Prince hears Snow White singing while she cleans. He falls in love with her voice before he even meets her.

The Magic Mirror informs the Queen that Snow White is the fairest in the land. The Queen orders the Huntsman to kill the princess, but instead he tells her to run away.

Snow White hides in a cottage owned by the Seven Dwarfs. When they arrive home to find a stranger inside, they are afraid. But they soon build a wonderful friendship with Snow White and come to love her.

🌿 Poisonous plan

Disguised as an ugly old peddler woman, the Queen persuades trusting Snow White to take one bite of the poisoned apple. She promises this will make all her dreams come true.

The Prince never gave up searching for Snow White.

As soon as Snow White takes a bite of the apple, she falls to the ground in a deep sleep and cannot be woken. When the Dwarfs find her, they place her in a special glass casket and keep a vigil at her side.

🌿 To the palace

The Prince wakes Snow White from her slumber with true love's kiss. Together, they set off into the sunset.

Cinderella

From the moment her beloved father dies, Cinderella's life changes forever. Before she knows it, she is forced to work as a servant to her cruel stepmother and stepsisters, who make her life miserable. However, Cinderella never loses hope that one day her life will change.

Helping hand

Although they are only tiny mice, Gus and Jaq are Cinderella's loyal friends. They help with her chores and save her from being lonely.

About Cinderella

★ She is brave and strong-willed, no matter how difficult things are.

★ Cinderella is hardworking and practical.

★ She is very caring, and her heart is full of kindness.

Fairy Godmother

The Fairy Godmother makes Cinderella's dreams of happiness come true. Her magic spell makes it possible for Cinderella to go to the ball, even if it is only for a few hours.

Her clothes

Cinderella has no money to spend on clothes. Her animal friends help patch up her simple dress and apron each morning and shine her worn-out shoes.

Headband matches her gown

Puffy sleeves

Elegant evening gloves

The birds and mice sew frills and bows on an old dress that once belonged to her mother so that Cinderella can go to the ball.

If you tell a wish, it won't come true.

Long, flowing skirt, made of shimmering sky-blue satin

Cinderella dances with Prince Charming, wearing a beautiful ball gown created by the Fairy Godmother.

Delicate lace petticoat

Home sweet home

Once upon a time, the chateau was the happiest place in the entire kingdom. But when Cinderella's mean stepmother arrives, things change. Lady Tremaine makes Cinderella sleep in the attic and do household chores all day long.

While Cinderella's father was alive, the house was full of warmth and laughter. Cinderella was happy.

❄ Home life

Cinderella can see the royal castle from her bedroom window, and she imagines how wonderful it would be to live there.

Every morning, Cinderella feeds the animals before she takes breakfast up to Lady Tremaine in bed.

❄ Family and friends

Jaq and Gus care deeply for Cinderella. The same cannot be said for her stepfamily. She waits on them hand and foot without any thanks!

❄ The family

Lady Tremaine and her spoiled daughters, Drizella and Anastasia, hate Cinderella because of her natural beauty.

Lucifer the cat lies in wait to torment the mice. Even Cinderella, who loves most animals, hasn't a good word to say about him!

Cinderella's
tiny attic
bedroom

Steep staircase
leads up to
Cinderella's
bedroom

The kitchen
where Cinderella
spends much of
her day cooking
and cleaning

Magic makeover

A little magic is all Cinderella needs to find her happy ever after. She has charm and beauty and all the elegance of a princess, and with a little help from her Fairy Godmother, her dreams come true.

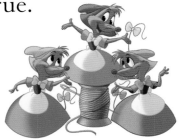

The mice help Cinderella get ready for the ball.

The invitation

To celebrate the Prince's return, all eligible ladies in the land are invited to attend a ball at the castle.

Torn apart

Cinderella's ugly stepsisters cannot bear to see her looking so beautiful in her mother's dress. They are so jealous that they tear her outfit to pieces.

A touch of magic

With a wave of her magic wand, the Fairy Godmother ensures that Cinderella can go to the ball.

The ball

As soon as they see each other, Cinderella and the Prince fall in love. But when the clock strikes twelve, Cinderella leaves her glass slipper behind in her hurry to leave before the magic ends.

Cinderella's golden hair is swept up.

Ball gown sparkles in the light

Mixed feelings

The Grand Duke is absolutely delighted when Cinderella produces the matching glass slipper and slips it on to her dainty foot. Lady Tremaine, on the other hand, is furious.

After all his searching, Prince Charming has at last found the enchanting girl he danced with at the ball. The whole kingdom rejoices when he marries Cinderella.

Sleeping Beauty

Brought up in the countryside, this sweet, gentle girl has no idea that she is really a princess named Aurora. She learns the truth on her sixteenth birthday, the same day that, due to a curse put on her as a baby by a wicked fairy, she falls into an enchanted sleep. Only true love's kiss saves her from eternal slumber.

About Aurora

★ She's cheerful and embraces her simple life in the forest.

★ Aurora is thoughtful and always willing to help.

★ She is a dreamer, and she's not shy about expressing her hopes for the future.

✦ Her favorite things

As a baby, Aurora was given the gift of song. Her voice is sweet and pure, and she loves to sing to the animals in the forest.

*If you **dream** a thing more than once, it's sure to **come true**!*

Elegant dress, fit for a princess

Aurora lives in a cottage in the heart of a beautiful forest. The woods are her playground where she can think and dream, dip her toes in the stream, and pick sweet berries.

Her hair is the color of golden sunshine.

✳ Her clothes

Growing up in the forest, Aurora has a simple wardrobe. She looks lovely even in the plainest of dresses with just a shawl to wrap around her shoulders.

Flora insists that Aurora's dress should be pink.

✳ The good fairies

When an evil fairy, Maleficent, curses Aurora, her parents send her to live with the good fairies Flora, Fauna, and Merryweather in the woods. They rename the girl Briar Rose.

The fairies use their magic to make Aurora a stunning birthday dress. But should it be pink or blue? They can't decide!

✳ A dress for a princess

When Aurora returns to her home at the royal palace, she wears a more refined dress and a golden crown.

Forest life

The good fairies take baby Aurora to live in a pretty little cottage, deep in the forest, to hide her from the wicked fairy's curse. They rename her Briar Rose after the wild flower that grows in the forest, and they live here happily for sixteen years.

✴ Birthday celebrations

Unlike most princesses, who have servants, Briar Rose begins her birthday by helping her aunts dust and spring-clean their little cottage! She loves the simple life in her woodland home.

Flora, Fauna, and Merryweather love Briar Rose dearly and have special plans for her birthday. They ask her to pick berries in the forest so that they can make her a surprise gift.

Briar Rose meets the man of her dreams in the forest, and her birthday is the happiest ever. She doesn't realize that the handsome young man is actually a prince.

Sparks of blue and pink magic escape from the chimney.

Roof made of straw

The little birds love to visit Briar Rose in her bedroom.

Red, brick chimney

In the castle

The baby princess was named Aurora after the dawn because, like a new day, she brought sunshine into her parents' lives. The King and Queen threw a party at the palace in celebration, but it was interrupted by the wicked fairy, Maleficent. She promised that Aurora would prick her finger on a spindle and die before the sun set on her sixteenth birthday.

At the party, King Hubert and King Stefan celebrate the betrothal of their children, Phillip and Aurora.

Baby celebrations

Flora and Fauna bless Aurora with gifts of song and beauty. Merryweather uses her gift to alter Maleficent's curse.

The secret chamber where Aurora sleeps peacefully

Maleficent is very offended when she is not invited to the royal party. She is so angry that she curses the baby Aurora.

The fire dies down to reveal a secret door to the tower.

The spell draws Aurora to this spinning wheel.

✦ Sixteen years later

Maleficent's curse comes into effect when Aurora pricks her finger on a spinning wheel and falls into a deep sleep. When Prince Phillip tries to save Aurora, Maleficent turns into a fierce dragon—but with the Sword of Truth and Shield of Virtue, he defeats her.

Breaking the curse

Aurora lives in the forest with the three good fairies, who are charged with protecting her from Maleficent's curse. Aurora has been safe and happy for sixteen years, but she longs for excitement. On her sixteenth birthday, her life changes beyond anything she could have imagined.

✴ Powerful fairy

Maleficent's curse is very powerful. Merryweather can't undo it, but she can change it, so that if Aurora pricks her finger she will fall into an enchanted sleep.

✴ Woodland dance

Just before her sixteenth birthday, Briar Rose meets Prince Phillip in the woods. Little does either one know that they met once before— when Aurora was a baby!

Briar Rose is upset when the fairies tell her that she is a princess. She doesn't want to marry a prince she has never met! She doesn't realize that she has already met and fallen in love with the prince.

Golden crown is a present from the fairies.

✸ Birthday curse

As soon as Aurora pricks her finger on the spindle, she feels dizzy and falls into a deep sleep.

We've met before.
Once upon a dream!

Prince Phillip wears a red cape.

Royal tunic

When the fairies find Aurora asleep, they know that the King and Queen will be heartbroken.

The floaty skirt makes her feel like she's dancing on air.

✸ The broken spell

When Phillip kisses Aurora, Maleficent's curse is broken, and she wakes from her sleep.

Ariel

Ariel is a beautiful mermaid princess. She loves her father and older sisters, but she dreams of exploring the human world. Ordinarily, merpeople cannot live above the water, but Ariel is determined to find a way. Young and headstrong, this curious mermaid is always up for an adventure.

About Ariel

⭐ She's adventurous, free-spirited, and loves to explore.

⭐ Impulsive and curious, Ariel goes where the current takes her.

⭐ Ariel is funny and brave.

Flounder

Ariel's best friend is a little fish named Flounder. They go on many exciting adventures together and often end up in lots of trouble!

Scuttle

Ariel consults her funny seagull friend, Scuttle, about all human things. He claims to be an expert!

Sebastian

Sebastian is Triton's loyal crab composer and is supposed to watch over Ariel. He tries hard but finds it difficult to keep up with her.

Pale-green fins

🐚 Exploring

Ariel loves to collect human objects she finds on sunken ships and the ocean floor. She stores her collection of treasures in a secret underwater grotto, close to the palace.

Red hair floats in the water

Powerful mermaid tail helps her swim fast

Even if it means swimming into dangerous, shark-infested waters, Ariel cannot resist the temptation to explore the ocean for shipwrecks so that she can add to her amazing collection of human objects.

🐚 King of the sea

King Triton cannot understand his youngest daughter's love for humans. He thinks that they are dangerous and forbids her from exploring.

*I don't see how a world that makes such **wonderful things** could be bad!*

Under the sea

Deep under the ocean is a marvelous world of brightly colored fish, corals, seaweeds, and a sparkling palace that is home to King Triton and his mermaid daughters. But danger lurks underwater, too, if only Ariel would listen.

Palace in the deep

Ariel lives in a spectacular sea palace, but the only treasures she's impressed by are those she collects from the human world. She knows her father will be angry if he finds out about her secret collection.

Ariel and her sisters' bedroom

King Triton's magnificent throne room

Palace is built from sea coral

Ariel shares her bedroom with her six older sisters named Aquata, Andrina, Arista, Attina, Adella, and Alana. Sometimes Ariel finds it hard to be the youngest because everyone treats her like a child!

Ursula

Ursula hates King Triton.
The octopus-like sea witch longs
to overthrow him so that she
can become Queen of the Sea.

Ursula's spies, Flotsam
and Jetsam, discover
that Ariel is in love with
Prince Eric and tell the sea witch.
Ursula uses this to her advantage
and offers to make Ariel a deal.

On dry land

Ursula uses her magic to make Ariel human, and, in exchange, Ariel gives up her beautiful voice. To stay human, Ariel must kiss Eric within three days. If she fails, she will belong to Ursula. To make things worse, Ursula disguises herself and tries to use Ariel's stolen voice to make Eric marry her instead! Ariel gathers her sea friends and leads the way to rescue Eric and save the day.

Prince Eric

Ariel sees Prince Eric for the first time as his magnificent ship sails past. It is the prince's birthday, and the crew celebrates with fireworks.

A violent storm throws the prince overboard, but Ariel rescues him and takes him to the shore. She falls deeply in love with Eric but must return to the sea.

Dress made from material found on the beach!

Turning human

As soon as Ariel drinks Ursula's magic potion, her tail disappears, and in its place are two legs! Now that she's a human, she can no longer breathe underwater.

Ariel has never had feet before!

🐚 A day to explore

Even without her voice, Ariel loves spending the day with Eric in his human kingdom. They take a carriage ride and even visit the town square together.

🐚 Royal wedding

When King Triton sees how much Ariel and Prince Eric love each other, he allows them to get married.

Without a voice, it is difficult for Ariel to communicate with Eric and his manservant, Grimsby.

Ariel's bedroom

The town

Roof garden

Eric's ship

The sea view from the dining room means Ariel is never far from home.

Belle

Belle knows that true beauty lies within. But even her goodness is tested when she first sets eyes on the hideous-looking beast who lives in the enchanted castle. Although she doesn't know it, Belle's loving nature and intelligence have the power to transform the Beast into a handsome prince.

About Belle

⭐ She longs for adventure and is very brave.

⭐ She's smart and makes her own judgments.

⭐ She is imaginative and loves to read stories.

🌹 Sweet escape

Belle's only true friends in the village are the heroes and heroines she meets in the books she loves to read.

I've just finished a wonderful story!

🌹 Family comes first

Although some people in the village think that Maurice is just a foolish old man, Belle has total faith in her father.

Long, silky hair is the color of chocolate

Big brown eyes are full of warmth

Simple, white blouse

Basket is great for carrying books!

Practical blue dress

🌹 Castle friends

Lumière and Cogsworth are two of the castle servants who are changed into household objects by the enchantress. They hope Belle will help them turn back into humans again.

Mrs. Potts, the kindly cook, and Chip, her playful son, cheer Belle up when she first arrives.

🌹 Special clothes

At the castle, the helpful Wardrobe provides Belle with all the clothes she could possibly need during her stay.

Although it is snowing, Belle likes being outdoors. The Wardrobe provides a warm cloak that Belle wears for a walk with the Beast in the gardens.

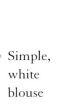

Enchanted castle

Belle and her father live on the edge of the town. When Maurice accidentally stumbles upon a mysterious castle in the forest, a whole new chapter in Belle's life begins.

When Gaston learns about the Beast he leads the villagers on a rampage through the forest to find his castle and destroy the Beast.

*B*elle feels different from the other people in her quiet village and she longs for adventure. Then one day, she discovers both magic and excitement in an enchanted castle that lies in the forest, just beyond her doorstep.

Snow-covered turrets

Disobeying orders

Belle is forbidden from entering the West Wing of the castle. That's where the enchanted rose is kept.

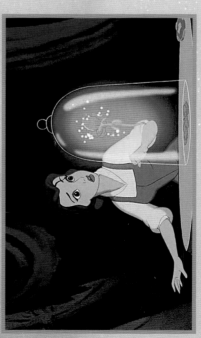

Enchanted rose

Castle kitchen

Belle and the Beast share a dance in the ball room.

The library is Belle's dream come true!

Belle has an unusual meal prepared for her.

Learning to love

Belle does not know it, but the Beast is actually a prince. He once refused shelter to a beggar woman (who was really an enchantress), and she turned him into a horrible beast. The spell can be broken only if the prince learns to love and be loved in return before the last petal of the enchanted rose falls.

Golden ball gown

Unsuitable partner

Gaston may be the most handsome man in town, but Belle is horrified at the thought of marrying such a vain and rude man.

A daughter's love

Belle loves her father so much that, although scared, she promises to stay in the Beast's castle forever so her father can be free.

The Enchantress offered a rose to the Beast in exchange for shelter from the cold.

Be our guest

The magical servants are overjoyed to welcome Belle to the enchanted castle. She is the first guest they have had in years!

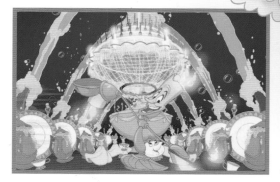

His true nature

When the Beast learns to control his temper, Belle sees the kind and loving person within.

The Beast and Belle develop a true friendship. The Beast grants Belle her freedom so she can help her father —even though he will lose his only chance to become human again. This act of kindness makes Belle realize how much she loves him.

Belle loves the Beast no matter what he looks like.

Gown has many layers underneath

Transformation

The Beast is terribly wounded by Gaston, and Belle fears she is too late to save him.

After Belle confesses her love for the Beast, the spell is broken. The Beast regains his appearance as a handsome prince, and all the enchanted objects become humans again.

Jasmine

Princess Jasmine wants to experience life beyond the palace. When she meets Aladdin, her world changes forever, and she realizes that she wants to marry only someone she loves. Although her father and the evil Jafar have other plans for her, Jasmine is not about to let them rule her life!

About Jasmine

⭐ Fiercely independent, she longs to be free and able to make her own choices.

⭐ She isn't afraid to stand up to Jafar and speak her own mind.

⭐ She's adventurous and intelligent.

❋ The Sultan

Jasmine's father is the Sultan of Agrabah. He has brought her up in a life of luxury and wants only the best for his daughter.

❋ Loyal friend

Rajah is Jasmine's pet tiger and her closest friend in the palace. She tells him all her secrets and dreams.

❋ Monkey mischief

At first, Abu is rude to Jasmine, but she soon becomes very fond of the cheeky monkey.

Sparkling saphire fixed to her headband

❋ Jafar

Jafar, the evil vizier and assistant to Jasmine's father, will never win her respect, no matter how powerful he is.

❋ No freedom

Jasmine hates not being free to go where she chooses. She decides to see for herself what life is like on the other side of the palace walls.

Jasmine is not impressed when her father introduces her to Prince Ali because she doesn't recognize Aladdin in his princely clothes. Jasmine is determined to choose a husband for herself.

Flowing turquoise silk pants

Aladdin may be poor, but to Jasmine, he is a prince.

Agrabah

Jasmine lives in the desert city of Agrabah, in a splendid palace with her father. It is a wonderful city of mystery and enchantment, but she has never been outside the palace walls. Jasmine longs to experience the noise and excitement of the lively city for herself.

✳ The palace

The palace is surrounded by lush gardens. But even in these beautiful gardens, Jasmine feels trapped and wants to see the city that lies beyond the palace walls.

The Sultan's palace

The dungeon is located underneath the palace. This is where Aladdin is held after he is arrested by Jafar's men.

In the throne room, there is a hidden door that leads up to Jafar's secret lair. He goes there to think up ways to overthrow the Sultan.

Jafar's secret lair

Aladdin's secret hideaway is on the rooftop of an old, abandoned building. He has amazing views of the whole city and can even see the Sultan's palace.

✳ The city

In the marketplace, Jasmine gives an apple to a hungry child without realizing she needs to pay for it. Aladdin saves her from the angry apple seller!

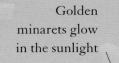

Golden minarets glow in the sunlight

✳ Cave of Wonders

In the desert, on the outskirts of the city, the Cave of Wonders appears. The cave is filled with precious jewels and treasures. It is here that Aladdin finds the Magic Lamp.

Magic adventures

It may not look like much on the outside, but when Aladdin rubs the dirty old lamp, an all-powerful Genie appears. The Genie can grant his new master three wishes and could make Aladdin as powerful as the Sultan. But all Aladdin wants is to marry Jasmine—and in the end, he doesn't need magic or the Genie to earn her love.

✽ The Genie

The Genie feels a little cramped inside the tiny lamp, his home for the last 10,000 years. He understands Jasmine's longing for freedom.

The Genie has amazing magical powers.

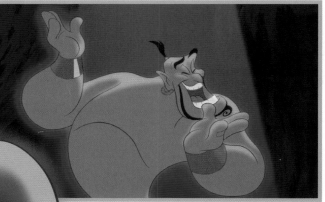

Like Jasmine, the Genie wants to be able to make his own choices and be his own master. Although the Genie is powerful, he can grant only other people's wishes—not his own.

✳ The Magic Carpet

The Magic Carpet can fly extremely fast!

Stuck in the Cave of Wonders, Aladdin and Abu might not have escaped without the Magic Carpet. Although shy and timid at first, the Carpet becomes their friend and helps them out of danger.

✳ Iago

Iago is Jafar's noisy, bad-tempered parrot. He helps Jafar carry out his evil plans.

✳ Three wishes

Aladdin uses his first wish selfishly. He wishes to become the wealthy Prince Ali. He uses his second wish to save his own life. Aladdin's last wish is to set the Genie free.

✳ Time's up

Jafar steals the Magic Lamp, and the Genie is forced to obey his evil wishes. Aladdin knows that Jafar craves power and cleverly tricks him into wishing to be a genie. Jafar's wish comes true, and he becomes trapped in the lamp forever.

I am not a prize to be won!

Pocahontas

Pocahontas is a member of the Powhatan tribe, and her name means "little mischief." She is a free spirit and very adventurous—she loves roaming the beautiful lands around her village. Pocahontas believes in listening to her own heart, and she dreams of great adventures just around the corner.

About Pocahontas

* She sees the beauty in nature.
* Pocahontas is determined to choose her own path in life.
* She is confident enough to stand up for what she believes in.

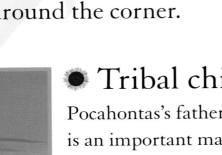

● Tribal chief

Pocahontas's father, Powhatan, is an important man. He must take care of the whole tribe and make difficult decisions.

When Pocahontas needs advice, she visits Grandmother Willow. The ancient talking tree is extremely wise.

The Powhatan tribe care for and respect the land they live on. They will do anything they can to keep it safe.

My dream is pointing me down another path.

Necklace belonged to Pocahontas's mother

Nakoma

Nakoma is Pocahontas's loyal and best friend. She often follows Pocahontas on her adventures, although she is not always willing to take the same risks!

Friends

Pocahontas is often joined on her adventures by Meeko, a curious raccoon, and Flit, a hummingbird who makes sure she's always safe.

Simple dress

Visitors

It seems that Pocahontas is right. Change is coming. English explorer Captain John Smith is sailing to the new world, hoping to make exciting discoveries in this unknown place.

Strong legs help her run fast

Meeting settlers

When John Smith and the other settlers arrive, Pocahontas is quite curious. She wants to see who they are and how they live. She tries to learn all about their world because it is so different to that of her tribe.

Pocahontas is always eager to explore new places and meet new people.

John Smith

At first, John Smith is not sure what to make of the new world. When he meets Pocahontas, she opens his eyes to the beauty of the land and its inhabitants.

This is the path I choose.

Fringed, tan dress

Greedy visitor

John Smith is working for Governor Ratcliffe, a greedy man who just wants wealth and power. He believes that Pocahontas and her tribe are hiding lots of valuable gold.

● Kocoum

Kocoum is a brave warrior. Pocahontas likes him, but she does not love him. Kocoum cares so much for Pocahontas that he dies trying to protect her.

● Gathering

Pocahontas's father, Chief Powhatan, is a great leader, but his people are afraid and worried about the settlers.

On the voyage to the new world, John Smith rescued a young man named Thomas during a storm. Thomas has been fiercely loyal to his friend John ever since.

John Smith's compass helps him find his way when he is lost. Pocahontas recognizes the spinning arrow from a dream about finding her own path.

● New greeting

John Smith shows Pocahontas how to shake hands. In exchange, she teaches him how she says "Hello" and "Goodbye" in her language.

Saying goodbye

Although John Smith and Pocahontas develop a strong bond, their people are unable to overcome their differences. John Smith is badly wounded and must return home on his ship, but he and Pocahontas will never forget each other.

● Brave

Pocahontas runs between her father and John Smith. She convinces her father to remember the path of peace and saves John Smith. Later, John Smith throws himself in the path of a bullet to save Chief Powhatan.

John Smith and Pocahontas are not the only ones who are making new friends. When Meeko meets Governor Ratcliffe's pampered pet dog, Percy, the unlikely pair become pals!

An injured John Smith bids farewell to Pocahontas. He promises to be with her forever in his heart.

Meeting in the middle

Pocahontas is courageous enough to put herself in the middle of the settlers and her own tribe. Her cry for peace prevents a war from breaking out.

Sailing away

Pocahontas runs to the top of the cliff where she first spotted the settlers' ship. Now she watches as John Smith leaves on his voyage back to England.

Pocahontas is sad to see John Smith sail away.

The ship is named *Susan Constant*.

At first glance, Pocahontas thought the sails were clouds.

Mulan

Mulan is strong and spirited, but she has the unfortunate habit of causing trouble without meaning to. She is devoted to her family and always helpful. But Mulan struggles to stay true to herself while bringing honor to her family.

About Mulan

★ Mulan is smart. She's great at solving problems.

★ She's loyal, both to her family and to her friends in the army.

★ Tough and strong, Mulan rarely gives up, even when the odds are against her.

✿ Loving family

Mulan's mother and grandmother think she should get married and take her to see a Matchmaker. If the Matchmaker likes Mulan, she will help her make a good marriage.

Don't worry, father. I won't let you down.

Although Mulan is not happy to be meeting the Matchmaker, she does her best because she loves her family. She tries to fit in and manages to look elegant, until things start to go wrong.

Mulan's meeting with the Matchmaker does not go well. She accidentally spills the tea, gives the Matchmaker an ink beard, and sets her on fire!

Hair that just won't stay neat!

At home, Mulan's best friends are a horse and dog, who look out for her and help her with the chores.

Traditional Chinese robe

Loyal friends

When Mulan starts her journey, some new friends accompany her—Mushu the dragon and the lucky Cri-kee.

Family honor

Mulan longs to bring honor to her family but doesn't know how. When her father is called to fight in the army, Mulan thinks he is too injured to make the trip.

Fearless daughter

Mulan wants to save her father, but joining the army is no easy task, especially when disguised as a man! But Mulan is determined to succeed and bring honor to her family. Although she has Mushu and Cri-kee by her side, her fellow new recruits don't seem very friendly. Still, Mulan works hard to win their respect.

Becoming Ping

In the middle of the night, Mulan steals her father's armor and sword. She disguises herself as a boy named Ping and takes his place in the army. It's a pretty daring plan!

Mushu wants to be a family guardian.

Hair cut short and tied in a high bun

Dangerous times

China is under threat from the invading Huns, so the Emperor calls up every available male into the army. The Emperor is a wise and great man, but his advisors are not so smart.

Mulan takes on a tough challenge: to climb a pole carrying heavy weights. She cleverly uses the weights to help her climb and is the only recruit to reach the top!

❀ Army captain

The soldiers are led by Captain Li Shang. He is tough and brave and wants his men to be just like him. Of course, he has no idea that one of his recruits is a woman.

At first, Mulan's fellow soldiers don't seem to like "Ping" very much, but "his" courage and strength win them over.

Mulan has to prove to Li Shang that "Ping" has what it takes to be a good soldier. She shows him through hard work she can do it.

How about a girl who has a brain, who always speaks her mind?

❀ Shan Yu

The Huns are led by the ruthless Shan Yu. However, Mulan's quick thinking saves Li Shang and the Emperor.

Proud warrior

Mulan's determination has turned her into a strong and brave soldier. She is more than a match for any man! That only makes it harder to bear when her true identity is revealed and Mulan is sent away from the army.

When she discovers the Huns at the Emperor's palace, Mulan uses her wits to find a way to save the Emperor.

❀ Hero

During a huge avalanche, Mulan risks her life to rescue her captain Li Shang.

❀ Courage

Even after she is forced to leave the army, Mulan proves to be filled with courage. She returns to save the day with a daring plan.

Mulan is confident wielding a sword.

Mulan is able to return home with honor and pride. Her father is just happy to see her! Having Mulan as a daughter is the greatest honor he could wish for.

🌸 Grateful Emperor

Mulan is shocked when everyone bows down to her. The Emperor never bows to anyone! He makes an exception for Mulan when she saves him—and his Empire—from the Huns.

🌸 Imperial City

Instead of punishing Mulan for her lie, the Emperor thanks her and honors her with a medal in front of huge crowds.

Fireworks light up the sky.

Emperor's palace

Tiana

Ambitious and hardworking, Tiana's dream is to run her own restaurant. However, that means working two jobs to save up enough money to make her dream come true. That doesn't leave her with much time to relax or spend time with her friends and family.

About Tiana

★ She loves cooking and is determined to open her own restaurant.

★ Independent Tiana doesn't need anyone to help make her dreams come true.

★ She knows exactly what she wants and works hard to achieve her goals.

🌿 Foodie

Food has always been an important part of Tiana's life, thanks to her father, James.

Tiana is wearing one of Charlotte's many dresses.

🌿 Best friend

Tiana's best friend is Charlotte LaBouff. The two girls' lives couldn't be more different. Charlotte's dad gets her everything she wants.

This crown is
only pretend.

Important visitor

Prince Naveen of Maldonia is the complete opposite
to Tiana. He loves parties and has never done a
day's work in his life! His greatest passion is jazz,
and he has come to New Orleans to make sweet
music and hopefully find a rich woman to marry!

Prince Naveen's parents are
tired of their son's party
lifestyle, so they disinherit
him. The pampered prince
needs to find a way to get
some money. Working for it is
out of the question, of course.

Blue sash tied
elegantly around
her skirt

Prince Naveen is guest of
honor at Charlotte's father's
costume party. Charlotte hopes
he will fall in love with her.
Tiana is just there to work.

A froggy business

Tiana is not interested in princes and fairy tales—that's Charlotte's dream. However, it is Tiana, not Charlotte, who finds herself caught up in a truly amazing story. A prince with a problem, some quirky creatures, and a sprinkling of magic are the recipe for adventure.

Prince charmed

Dr. Facilier promises to make Prince Naveen rich, but the mean magician turns him into a frog instead! Only a kiss from a princess can break the spell.

I'm not a princess. I'm a waitress.

Mistaken identity

At Charlotte's party, Tiana's outfit gets ruined, so she borrows one of Charlotte's dresses. When Naveen sees her, he thinks that he has found his princess and begs her for a kiss.

The kiss doesn't quite go as planned, and Tiana becomes a frog, too! The froggy pair make a quick escape from the party and head to the bayou.

🌿 Life in the bayou

Life as frogs isn't easy, but Naveen and Tiana make some good friends in the bayou. Louis is a jazz-loving alligator with a heart of gold.

Ray is a romantic firefly who shows the froggy pair that anything is possible, if it's true love.

🌿 True love

It's certainly not love at first sight, but as Tiana teaches Naveen about hard work, he teaches her about the other important things in life.

Tiana and Naveen grow closer in the bayou as their adventure shows them what really matters in life.

Magical Mama Odie tells them that to be happy and become human again, they must find out what they need, not what they want.

Princess Tiana

Tiana and Naveen get to know each other as frogs and eventually realize that they can't live without each other. When it seems like they might never be human again, the perfect pair decide that just being together is enough for them.

Tough choice

Tiana and Naveen are ruining Dr. Facilier's schemes. He offers Tiana a restaurant, if she will betray Naveen. But Tiana finally understands what she needs and rejects his offer.

My dream wouldn't be complete without you in it.

Naveen has learned what he needs, too—Tiana. And he would do anything for her.

True love

Charlotte knows true love when she sees it and offers to kiss Naveen to break the spell. But she is too late.

As a frog, Prince Naveen has to kiss a princess to break the spell and become human again. This doesn't happen until he and Tiana marry. When the frog prince kisses his frog bride, Tiana becomes a princess, and the spell is broken at last.

Lily-pad tiara

Jeweled necklace

Long, pale-green gloves

New dreams

Tiana never dreamed of becoming a princess, but she certainly likes being one now! As for Naveen, a little time as a frog makes him a much better prince. Now they both like the idea of spending more time together … forever!

After their froggy wedding, Tiana and Naveen get remarried. Their family and friends all join them to celebrate, and Charlotte catches Tiana's bouquet!

Tiana's Palace

Tiana's love of cooking began when she was a little girl, and she used to cook bowls of gumbo with her father. Now she works as a waitress, saving up all her money until she can buy her own place. When that day comes, Tiana will use everything she has learned to make her restaurant the best in town.

Tiana works the day shift at Duke's Diner and the night shift at Cal's. She is a busy girl!

Writing pad to take orders

Big dreams

Tiana first dreamed of having her own restaurant when she was a little girl and shared her plans with her father, James. He always encouraged her to follow her dreams.

Customers can be very demanding, but Tiana is a good waitress and knows how to do lots of things at once.

🌿 Dreams come true

After a lot of hard work and a little bit of magic, Tiana finally opens her own place. And with Naveen by her side, it is even better than she dreamed it would be.

At Tiana's restaurant, everyone is welcome—kings, queens, and her new friends from the bayou.

When she was a child, Tiana dreamed of calling her restaurant Tiana's Place. Now that she is grown up and a princess, she thinks Tiana's Palace is a better name!

Rapunzel

Rapunzel has no idea that she is a princess who was kidnapped as a baby. She has spent the last eighteen years living inside a tower with Gothel, who she thinks is her mother. That's all about to change when Rapunzel tries to find the source of the floating lights that appear in the sky every year on her birthday.

Young princess

The King and Queen loved their daughter very much and have been very sad since she was taken. Every year on her birthday, they release lanterns in her memory.

About Rapunzel

* She is curious to learn about the world outside her tower.
* When she sets her sights on something, she is fearless, and nothing can hold her back.
* She has endless creative hobbies.

Simple, homemade dress

Long, magical hair takes three hours to brush.

Magical hair

Wicked Gothel took Rapunzel as a baby. The princess's hair contains magic that keeps Gothel looking young and beautiful.

Her hair is 70 feet (21 meters) long.

✳ Keeping busy

Gothel doesn't let Rapunzel ever leave the tower, so the energetic young girl has to find ways to amuse herself.

When I promise something, I never ever break that promise.

One of Rapunzel's favorite hobbies is painting. She finds lots of ways to express herself while she's bored in the tower.

Rapunzel likes to keep fit by stretching and exercising. But it is no substitute for the feeling of grass beneath her feet.

The secret tower

Gothel has hidden Rapunzel well. The scheming lady chose a secret tower in the middle of a mysterious valley. It has no front door, so Gothel uses Rapunzel's long hair as a ladder when she wants to get in or out of the tower.

For eighteen years no one has found them, until now …

Window from
which Rapunzel
lets down her hair

❋ Visitor

Lovable rogue Flynn Rider is being chased when he stumbles upon the tower. He thinks it will be a great place to hide.

Flynn climbs the outside of the tower, and Rapunzel welcomes him with a frying pan to the face!

Plants growing on the tower make it even tougher to climb.

✳ Free at last

At first, Rapunzel is suspicious of Flynn, until she realizes he can help her leave the tower. Finally, Rapunzel is going to see what is out there!

Gothel has never told Rapunzel, but there is a trapdoor in the floor hiding a secret staircase. It leads to the outside world.

New people

The only person Rapunzel ever sees is Mother Gothel. She lives a very sheltered life, and her only friend is a chameleon named Pascal. Gothel has always told her that the outside world is filled with frightening things. However, when Flynn Rider enters her life, Rapunzel finally escapes from the tower. Was Gothel right about life outside?

 ## Friends

Pascal can't talk, but he changes color to reflect his mood. He is a loyal friend to Rapunzel.

Maximus is a horse with the Palace Guard. He is strong and brave but a pushover for Rapunzel's sweet talking.

At first, Flynn's charms don't work on Rapunzel, but later they grow to like each other. Flynn even risks his life to save Rapunzel.

The regulars at the Snuggly Duckling pub look scary, but they all have a dream, just like Rapunzel.

Enemies

The Stabbington twins are double trouble. The brothers help Gothel find Rapunzel, but they are really looking for Flynn Rider.

Magical hair has never been cut

Time to be free

Rapunzel is not used to the outside world, but she can't stay locked in a tower forever, no matter what Gothel thinks!

Rapunzel doesn't wear shoes.

Gothel will stop at nothing to keep Rapunzel and her magical hair all to herself. Without Rapunzel's hair to keep her young, Gothel starts to look her true age.

Royal emblem of a shining sun

Haven't any of you ever had a dream?

Home at last

Leaving the tower is the best thing that has ever happened to Rapunzel. She is finally free to make new friends, fall in love, and, best of all, go home to her real parents.

Something special

Flynn helps Rapunzel enjoy her best-ever birthday. She realizes that he is a very special person.

Handy pouch for paint supplies

In the outside world, Rapunzel's hair can get easily tangled, so she finds a stylish solution to keep it out of the way.

✺ Magic lanterns

Rapunzel has always wanted to see the mesmerizing lanterns that are released every year on her birthday.

They may come from different worlds, but Rapunzel has never had more fun than when she's with Flynn.

Rapunzel finds out that the lanterns are for her! Her parents never stopped hoping for her return.

To save Rapunzel from Gothel and allow her to be free forever, Flynn cuts off Rapunzel's magical hair. Now her hair is short and dark, but that's just fine with her!

I'm the lost princess.

✺ Reunited

The King and Queen never gave up hope that they would find their long-lost daughter again. All three are overjoyed to be reunited at last.

Merida

Merida loves adventure and often spends her days riding through the Scottish forests with her horse, Angus. Fearless and curious, she also loves her freedom. When her parents call upon suitors to compete for Merida's hand in marriage, Merida fights for the right to choose her own path in life. Nobody tells this girl what to do!

About Merida

* She's not afraid to break tradition.
* Strong and athletic, she can ride a horse and shoot arrows at the same time.
* She is confident and strong-willed.

Royal family

Merida is close to her family but still wants to make her own choices, especially when it comes to choosing— or not choosing—a husband.

King Fergus

A loud and happy king, Fergus adores his family. Long ago he lost one of his legs in a fight with the bear Mor'du.

Unruly, fiery-red hair

Queen Elinor

The queen is elegant and ladylike, and she often butts heads with her daughter, Merida. Both mother and daughter are strong-willed, so when they disagree, the consequences can be serious.

Merida has been shooting a bow and arrow since she was six.

Triple trouble

Merida's triplet brothers, Harris, Hubert, and Hamish, are curious and mischievous. They'll do almost anything for sweets.

True friends

When she is alone with her horse Angus, Merida feels as if she can conquer the world.

Highland Games

Queen Elinor and King Fergus invite neighboring Lords Macintosh, MacGuffin, and Dingwall to their kingdom of DunBroch for the Highland Games. The purpose of the games is for the lords' sons to compete for Merida's hand in marriage. Merida is not at all happy about this, and she chooses archery as the challenge to determine her betrothed. Then she enters and wins the contest herself!

🍂 Macintosh

Lord Macintosh is both proud and sensitive. His son, Young Macintosh, shares that pride and often comes across as arrogant.

🍂 Dingwall

Lord Dingwall is quick-tempered and scrappy, while his son, Wee Dingwall, is quite the opposite. He enters the contest only to please his father.

🍂 MacGuffin

Both Lord MacGuffin and his son are extremely strong. Young MacGuffin is usually quiet, but when he speaks, almost nobody can understand his Scottish accent.

True to herself

The queen wants Merida to look like a princess. But Merida doesn't want to hide her hair or her personality. When her mom isn't looking, she lets her hair free.

The right to compete

As the firstborn of DunBroch, Merida declares that she has the right to compete in the archery contest. The crowds who have gathered to watch the Games are more than a little surprised!

I'll be shooting for my own hand.

Decorations on wooden bow

Bull's-eye!

Wee Dingwall hit a bull's-eye, but Merida hits it again, splitting his arrow.

Magical discoveries

Merida and her mother love each other, but lately they can't seem to get along. After yet another fight, Merida begs a mysterious witch for a spell to change the way her mother sees the world. The Witch gives Merida a cake for Elinor that turns the queen into a bear! Mother and daughter must work together to try to reverse the spell before it's too late.

🍂 Flickering guides

When Merida spots some magical will o' the wisps in the forest, she cannot help herself. She follows them with a wary Angus at her heels.

🍂 The spell

The wisps lead Merida to a spooky-looking cottage where she finds a witch. Merida thinks she has found the solution to her problem at home when the witch gives her a spell cake.

Merida offers the harmless-looking spell cake to her mom as a peace offering. The result is not so peaceful!

To undo the spell on her mother, Merida must solve the Witch's riddle to "mend the bond torn by pride." Desperately, she tries to repair the family tapestry she tore.

❦ A new look

The queen tries to look elegant, but her crown doesn't fit on her new bear head.

Arms held in dainty pose

❦ Mor'du

Their travels lead Merida and Elinor to the terrifying and monstrous bear, Mor'du. Merida faces the bear, but she is grateful that her mom-bear is there to help her.

Sorry, I don't **speak bear.**

Brave princess

Merida has struggled with her mother, but she definitely doesn't want her to get hurt! When she realizes that her mother is in danger, Merida is prepared to do anything she can to save her. In turn, she has won her mother's understanding. Their love for each other repairs the rift between them and reverses the spell just in time.

Castle DunBroch

Merida loves the stone walls and towers of the castle, as well as the beautiful landscape of DunBroch. But she wants to be free to explore it on her own.

Visitors are not surprised to see a large stuffed bear in the Great Hall of DunBroch. They don't know it's Queen Elinor!

Tall turrets

Stone walls are hundreds of years old

Lush, green hillsides

🍂 A fine fix

Merida tries to convince her father that the bear is in fact his wife, Elinor. She fears he might unknowingly kill the queen.

Merida stays brave even as her mother becomes more and more bearlike, and less like the queen she really is.

King Fergus is determined to protect his family, even if it means facing a terrifying bear again.

🍂 A loving bond

Merida only has to look inside to mend the bond with her mother. Their love and understanding of each other undoes the spell.

I just want you back, Mummy!

Elinor is impressed by Merida's bravery.

Merida sees her mother in a new light.

Moana

Moana lives on the island of Motunui with her father, Chief Tui, and her mother, Sina. Ever since she was a toddler, Moana has been drawn to the ocean. In fact, the ocean has chosen her to return the long-lost mystical heart to the goddess Te Fiti, the "mother island."

About Moana

* Strong and determined, Moana is a voyager and leader.
* She's compassionate and has a big heart.
* Moana willingly takes on new challenges.

Future chief

Moana is the daughter of the island chief, and she knows she is destined to become chief herself one day. It's a big responsibility for a sixteen-year-old girl to think about!

Gramma Tala

Moana shares a special bond with her grandmother Tala. They love dancing together with the waves. She encourages Moana to listen to the voice inside her.

Necklace holds the Heart of Te Fiti

The ocean calls

Moana's parents tell her not to go beyond the reef, but Moana yearns to go far beyond that. She dreams of traveling across the sea—it's calling to her.

Strong arms, capable of sailing for hours

Skirt made of pandanus leaves

The ocean washed up the Heart of Te Fiti for Moana when she was young. According to Gramma Tala, it is the life source of islands, vegetation, and nature.

Even as a toddler, Moana showed her innate kindness, offering a bit of shelter to a tiny turtle returning to the sea.

The ocean is a friend of mine.

Motunui

Long ago, the beautiful island of Motunui thrived, but now a mysterious darkness threatens it. Moana is determined to carry out her grandmother's dying wish that she save her island. Though her father thinks it is dangerous, she is drawn to the adventure as well as the hope of helping her people.

Inspiring ancestors

Moana is overjoyed to discover that, centuries before her birth, her ancestors were voyagers.

Golden
sandy beach

Hut where
Moana was
taught as a child

An amazing discovery

When Gramma Tala explains that Moana's ancestors were voyagers, Moana finds it hard to believe, until she visits a cave and sees the old ships for herself.

Meeting Maui

Maui is a demigod who stole the heart of Te Fiti. Moana needs his help to return the heart to Te Fiti. But he's not exactly eager to join her.

Clear turquoise-colored sea

Coconut palms provide food

Ocean journey

Moana has many challenges to overcome on her voyage. She must sail in stormy waters, outsmart pirates, and battle a sea monster—all in her very first trip away from home. Yet her biggest challenge is learning to trust her inner voice. Luckily, Moana has some friends to help her out along the way.

❀ Monster crab

Tamatoa is a giant monster crab. He is obsessed with shiny objects, which he collects and protects jealously. One of these objects is Maui's precious and powerful fishhook.

The ocean chose me.

❀ Te Ka

Te Ka is made up of red-hot lava and fire. The molten monster is the most dangerous foe Moana and Maui face.

These little Kakamora bandits dress in armor made of coconuts. They are fierce fighters who want to take the Heart of Te Fiti from Moana.

✿ Wave whisperer

As a tiny girl, Moana makes friends with the ocean. When she finally ventures out of Motunui, the ocean guides her and helps her on her journey. The waves are always on her side.

When they first meet, Maui steals Moana's boat. Eventually, they sail together on it. Maui proves himself to be a true friend to Moana.

Brown spots on mostly white hair

✿ Pua

Adorable piglet Pua is quite the loyal pet to Moana. He follows her everywhere.

✿ Heihei

Heihei is not the smartest rooster on Motunui. It is entirely by accident that he sets off on the voyage with Moana!

Wobbly legs

Finding her way

Not only is Moana born to become chief of her island, but she has also proved herself for this role. She has shown strength, courage, compassion, and tenacity. Although she is only sixteen years old, she has already shown that she has the virtues to become a wonderful chief.

Gramma Tala's advice

When Moana is at her lowest point, wondering how to return the heart of Te Fiti, Gramma Tala appears as a stingray and inspires her not to give up.

I will sail across the sea and restore the Heart of Te Fiti.

Determined

Despite the odds against her, Moana never ever gives up. She is determined to return the Heart of Te Fiti and bring life back to her island.

Maui uses his magical fishhook to shape-shift into different animals.

🌺 Heart held high

Instead of fighting Te Ka, Moana once again shows her kindness. She understands that Te Ka is really Te Fiti—this is what she became without her glowing heart.

When Moana at last returns to the beachy shores of Motunui, she is greeted by her parents and the rest of the grateful people of her island.

🌺 Te Fiti

When Moana restores her heart, the glorious goddess Te Fiti transforms back to her natural, green, life-giving self. She is forever grateful to Moana.

Flowered headdress ~

Moana may have disobeyed her father by going beyond the reef, but her parents are proud of her and overjoyed to see her home.

Happily ever after

The royal adventures are at an end—for now. All of the princesses have learned that being a princess is not as easy as you might think. They have broken spells, overcome some impossible obstacles, shown great courage, and found true friendship, love, and happiness along the way. They may have ended their stories for now, but their tales live on inside every one of us, helping us to be as kind, brave, curious, and strong as they are!

How well do you know the princesses?

Now that you have read all about the adventures of the princesses, take this quiz to see how well you really know each one!

2. Which evil fairy curses Aurora when she is a baby?
a) Merryweather
b) Maleficent
c) Fauna

1. Which demigod helps Moana on her voyage?
a) Gramma Tala
b) Kakamora
c) Maui

3. Who is Jasmine's closest friend in the palace?
a) Rajah
b) Iago
c) Jafar

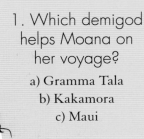

4. What pretend name does Mulan use when she disguises herself as a man?
a) Ping
b) Li Shang
c) Ling

5. Merida's mother is turned into which animal after eating a spell cake?
a) Badger
b) Wolf
c) Bear

6. What does Ariel give to Ursula in exchange for having human legs?

    a) Her voice
    b) Her treasures
    c) Her hair

7. What is Belle's favorite pastime?

    a) Writing
    b) Reading
    c) Baking

8. Which poisoned fruit does Snow White take a bite of?

    a) Gooseberry
    b) Cherry
    c) Apple

9. What does Cinderella leave on the palace stairs?

    a) A glass slipper
    b) A crystal tiara
    c) A diamond earring

10. Who is Pocahontas's raccoon friend?

    a) Flit
    b) Nakoma
    c) Meeko

11. What is Tiana's lifelong dream?

    a) To open a restaurant
    b) To marry a prince
    c) To kiss a frog

12. When does Rapunzel see floating lights in the sky?

    a) Every Thursday
    b) On her birthday each year
    c) On Gothel's birthday

Answers: 1c 2b 3a 4a 5c 6a 7b 8c 9a 10c 11a 12b